The Spencer School Sleepover

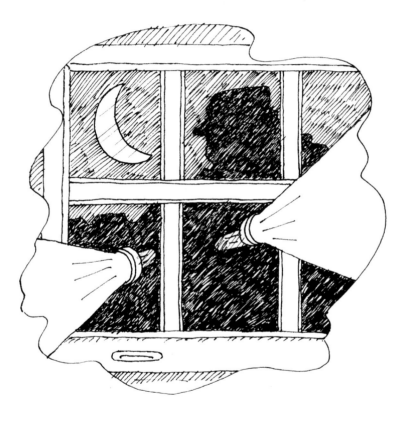

By Lucy Floyd
Illustrated by John Magine

The Spencer School Sleepover
Copyright ©2000 Wright Group/McGraw-Hill
Text by Lucy Floyd
Illustrations by John Magine

SUNSHINE™ is a trademark of Wright Group/McGraw-Hill.

Wright Group/McGraw-Hill
19201 120th Avenue NE, Suite 100
Bothell, WA 98011
www.WrightGroup.com

Printed in China through Colorcraft Ltd., Hong Kong

10 9 8 7 6 5 4 3

ISBN: 0-322-01798-X
ISBN: 0-322-01841-2 (6-pack)

CONTENTS

Spencer
School

Come to the Spencer School Sleepover

Friday at 6:00 p.m.
Activities
Games
Food
Join the fun!

CHAPTER 1
Sleep Well

"Now don't be nervous, Conrad," said Mom. "You're going to have fun tonight at the sleepover."

It was time for the annual Spencer School Sleepover. But Conrad was still trying to think of a way to back out of it.

"There'll be more than a hundred kids sleeping overnight in the school," Mom went on cheerfully, "and a lot of your classmates will be there."

"Yeah," said Conrad gloomily, "including Leapfrog Delaney."

Leapfrog got his name because he could jump so high. He was a whiz on the basketball court. "And Lilith and Halima, too," Conrad added.

"Well," said Mom, "I know those three stick together—"

"Like glue," said Conrad.

"—and they don't always include you," Mom continued.

"They *never* include me," said Conrad angrily. "Just because I'm the shortest one in our class, they think I'm a baby. Leapfrog calls me 'cute little Conrad.'"

"Children can be unkind," said Mom. Then she smiled brightly. "But you're so smart, Conrad! Your report card is always perfect!"

"Smart doesn't cut it," said Conrad. "I'm too little."

"I don't think it's your size," Mom said gently. "I think you're just a little bit shy.

Maybe you could try to be more outgoing, Conrad. Talk to your friends more."

"What friends?" Conrad mumbled.

Mom didn't hear him. "Lots of parents will be there tonight to help out," she said, "and teachers, too. You'll enjoy all the activities."

"I guess," said Conrad.

All the way to the school, Mom chattered about what a great time Conrad would have if he would just let himself. Conrad wondered if she might be right. Maybe he *would* have some fun.

But then, as he stepped out of the car, he heard a familiar voice.

"Well, if it isn't 'cute little Conrad,'" said Leapfrog. He was grinning.

Lilith was right behind Leapfrog, smiling down at Conrad. And Halima was right behind Lilith.

"I see you brought your mommy," Halima said.

"Now that's exactly why I decided not to be one of the parent volunteers!" Mom whispered to Conrad. "I don't want them thinking of you as a baby! Bye, honey. See you in the morning."

"Hello, Conrad!" Mr. Porter, the principal, smiled at Conrad. "Glad you're joining us for the sleepover!"

"Hey, Conrad, look!" called Amal Akbar. "I brought my Diney!" Amal was only in kindergarten, but he lived on Conrad's street. He was clutching a huge, green stuffed dinosaur.

"I brought something, too," said a soft voice behind Conrad.

Conrad turned around and saw Jasmine. He liked Jasmine. She was in his class, and she was quiet, like him. She was also small for her age.

"Hi, Jasmine," said Conrad.

"I brought my little pink pillow," Jasmine whispered. "Please don't tell anybody, Conrad. I sleep with it every

night, and I was afraid I'd be lonely without it."

"Don't worry. I won't tell," Conrad whispered back.

Suddenly, Mr. Porter's voice boomed over the loudspeakers.

"Welcome to the Spencer School Sleepover! We have a really big evening ahead, folks! There are lots of activities for you tonight: art, music, storytelling, and much more. The computer lab will be open for games, and snacks and drinks will be served in the cafeteria.

"Each of you will have a choice of bedtimes. These are posted in the hall. When you decide to go to bed, you will be assigned to a classroom. A parent or teacher will be in each classroom. Please leave your sleeping bags in your lockers until you are ready to go to bed.

"For safety, we ask that you stay in your assigned classroom for the entire night. All doors and windows will be securely locked. So have fun and sleep well!"

Sleep well. Conrad would remember Mr. Porter's words more than once that night.

CHAPTER 2
Room 108

After Conrad and Jasmine had stuffed their sleeping bags and backpacks into their lockers, it was time to choose something to do.

"How about the magic show first?" suggested Conrad.

"Sounds good to me," replied Jasmine. "I think it's in Room 101."

The magician was Mr. Porter himself. He was wearing a black cape and a shiny top hat. He made a scarf and some flowers appear from nowhere and then disappear again. Then he made some coins float in midair.

They went to the art room next. Mr. Kwan helped them add to a mural about the sleepover. Conrad painted a picture of himself in his sleeping bag. Jasmine drew Mr. Porter doing magic.

Then they went to the music room for singing. The music teacher, Ms. Grippo, led them in singing "She'll Be Coming 'Round the Mountain" and other songs.

"That was fun," said Conrad. "But it made me hungry."

"Me, too," Jasmine said. "Let's go have a snack."

As they walked together to the cafeteria, Conrad realized that he was

having a much better time at the sleepover than he had expected. Having Jasmine with him made all the difference. And she actually seemed to like being with him.

"What about the computer lab next?" Jasmine asked as she nibbled on an apple. "We could play some games."

Conrad knew a lot about computers. "Sure," he said. "I'd like that."

But that was before he saw who was in the computer lab.

Leapfrog was sitting at one of the computers, poking wildly at the keyboard.

"This thing won't work," he whined loudly. "Somebody needs to fix it!"

Lilith and Halima were also at computers, but for once they ignored Leapfrog. Then Leapfrog saw Conrad.

"Hey, Conrad," he said in a low voice, "maybe you could help me out here, pal."

Pal, thought Conrad. Yeah, right. But he went over to Leapfrog's computer anyway. He pressed a few keys and had the computer game going in no time.

"There you go," he said to Leapfrog. But Leapfrog didn't say anything. Not one little thank you.

"Having problems, Leapfrog?" called Lilith sweetly. Halima was covering her mouth, trying not to laugh.

"No problem," said Leapfrog loudly, in his I-know-everything voice. "I got it going."

"I've sort of lost interest in computer games," Conrad said to Jasmine.

"Me, too," Jasmine said. "Let's go to storytelling."

Lilith's mother, Mrs. Shapiro, was dressed like an astronaut as she told a science fiction story. Conrad enjoyed hearing about the planet Grizzmak and the huge, bearlike creatures that lived there, but he could feel himself getting sleepy. He yawned and rubbed his eyes.

"I'm sleepy, too," said Jasmine. "Let's go get our room assignment."

They were assigned to Room 108. The room parent was Mrs. Akbar, Amal's mother. Amal was already asleep on the floor, holding his green dinosaur beside him.

"Don't worry about him. He sleeps like a log," said Mrs. Akbar fondly, smiling at Amal. "Nothing wakes that child."

Conrad and Jasmine found a spot near the back of the room. "I'll take out my pink pillow after the lights are out," Jasmine whispered.

As Conrad was unrolling his sleeping bag, he heard more students arriving at Room 108. He looked toward the door.

"Oh, no!" Conrad groaned.

Leapfrog, Lilith, and Halima were coming in the door.

"We'll sleep here by the door, in case of an emergency," said Leapfrog loudly, in his I'm-in-charge-here voice.

Conrad wondered what kind of emergency Leapfrog had in mind. But he was too sleepy to think about Leapfrog anymore.

"Lights out!" sang Mrs. Akbar.

As Conrad drifted off to sleep, he thought about what his mom had told him. She was right after all. He *was* having fun.

CHAPTER 3
Sweet Dreams

The sound ripped through the dark room like the roar of a wild beast.

Grr-ROAR! Grrr-GRRRR-ROAR!

Conrad rubbed his eyes and wondered what was happening. What was that noise? Where was he? On the planet Grizzmak?

Grr-ROAR! Grrr-GRRRR-ROAR!

He must be dreaming about the zoo, Conrad decided. But what kind of animal makes a sound like *that?*

Grr-ROAR! Grrr-GRRRR-ROAR!

Now Conrad was wide awake. Jasmine was sitting up nearby. She was hugging her pink pillow tightly.

"Conrad!" she whispered. "What's that noise?"

"WHAT IS IT!" screamed a voice that Conrad would know anywhere. It was Leapfrog, and he was running for the door. "I gotta get out of here!" he screeched.

"Now, wait!" said Mrs. Akbar as she turned on the lights. "Don't panic!"

By this time, everyone was awake and talking. Everyone except Amal, that is. He was sleeping soundly, hugging his green dinosaur.

Mr. Porter came stumbling in the door. "I thought I heard a strange noise," he said, blinking in the bright light.

"Yes," said Mrs. Akbar, "and I know exactly what it is. I hope you weren't alarmed, children. Well, I guess Leapfrog was alarmed. Where is he, anyway?"

"When I saw him, he was running down the hall toward the office," said Mr. Porter.

"Well, we'll have to go get him," said Mrs. Akbar. "But first, let me solve this mystery."

She went over to Amal's dinosaur and pushed a button.

Grr-ROAR! Grrr-GRRRR-ROAR!

"It was just Amal's dinosaur," she said. "He rolled over onto the sound button. And he slept through the whole thing!"

"Well, that's solved," said Mr. Porter. "Now we just have to find Leapfrog."

"There he is," said Conrad.

Leapfrog was peeking around the edge of the open doorway.

"I was…um…I just wanted a drink of water," he mumbled.

"Okay, back to sleep, everyone!" said Mrs. Akbar. "I moved Diney so Amal won't roll over on him again."

"Good night, boys and girls," said Mr. Porter as he left. "Sweet dreams."

The room was quiet again, and Conrad was soon asleep. But he didn't sleep long.

CHAPTER 4
New Sounds

This time Conrad woke up to a quieter sound. Whispers and rustling noises were coming from over by the door.

Conrad heard Halima say, "Well, we can't wake up Mrs. Akbar again."

Then Leapfrog said, "But I *know* it's something this time—come on!"

There were more rustling sounds, and Conrad could just barely see three dark figures tiptoeing out of the room.

What was Leapfrog up to now? Conrad decided to find out.

He tiptoed out into the hallway. He saw Leapfrog, Lilith, and Halima turn left around the corner at the end of the hall. Where were they going? And why?

Conrad scurried down the hall and peered around the corner. It looked like Leapfrog and the others were headed toward the food supply room next to the cafeteria.

Conrad heard Leapfrog whispering again: "He's in there! I saw him go in!" Then Leapfrog reached out and turned a key that was in the lock of the supply room door.

"Let's go get Mr. Porter," Leapfrog said.

Conrad wondered who Leapfrog had just locked in the room. But he had no time to think it over, because Leapfrog and Lilith and Halima were hurrying back up the hallway.

Conrad stayed where he was, flat against the wall. The other three came running past and went up the hallway toward the school office.

After a moment, Conrad followed them. He crouched down low outside the office door and listened.

Halima was saying, "Well, Mr. Porter's not here. What now, Leapfrog?"

"Well," replied Leapfrog, "now we call 911, that's what."

There were three beeps from the office phone, and then Leapfrog said, "I need the police, please!"

After a few seconds of silence, Conrad heard Leapfrog again.

"Hello, Officer Diaz," Leapfrog was saying in his TV-detective voice. "I heard a suspicious sound during our sleepover. But I have apprehended the intruder."

Conrad knew Officer Diaz. He and Conrad's dad played golf together. Sometimes Mr. Porter played, too. Officer Diaz took his work seriously. Conrad knew he wouldn't appreciate it if this turned out to be one of Leapfrog's jokes.

"I have him locked in the food supply room," Leapfrog went on. "Yes, I will notify the school officials, Officer. And I'll be waiting for you." He hung up the phone.

"We'd better go find Mr. Porter right away," said Halima nervously.

"Why? We have things under control," said Leapfrog. "And besides, we don't even know where Mr. Porter is. Come on, let's go up front and wait."

Conrad quickly hid around a corner as Leapfrog, Lilith, and Halima came out of the office and hurried off toward the front door. Conrad followed, careful not to be seen.

Leapfrog was in the lead, talking nonstop about how he knew a *real* emergency when he saw one, and how he was just asleep when that dumb dinosaur noise went off, and how they shouldn't let little kids bring those kinds of things into the school anyway.

Leapfrog was still talking when Officer Diaz unlocked the front door and stepped inside.

Officer Diaz was all business. He shone his flashlight at each of the three students and then quickly down the length of the hallway.

"Where's Porter?" Officer Diaz asked.

"Oh, he's here somewhere," said Leapfrog airily.

"Well, first things first," the officer said. "Let's go check the food supply room."

Leapfrog, Lilith, and Halima trailed behind Officer Diaz as he walked toward the back of the school. Conrad followed behind them all, still unseen.

When he reached the supply room, Officer Diaz turned the key, opened the door slowly, and looked inside.

"Hello, Porter," he said.

CHAPTER 5
Just a Bad Dream?

Mr. Porter was sitting in the food supply room, eating pretzels from a huge bag.

"Hello, Diaz," he said. "What brings you here?"

"This young man reported an intruder," said Officer Diaz, pointing his flashlight at Leapfrog. "I came to check it out."

"No kidding?" said Mr. Porter. He stared at Leapfrog.

"Yup," said Officer Diaz, "and it looks like you were the 'intruder.' He locked you in this room."

"He did, did he?" said Mr. Porter. "Well, I was just in here having a midnight snack."

"I thought it might be something like that," said Officer Diaz.

"Leapfrog," said Mr. Porter in a very stern voice, "do you suppose you and your two friends could go back to your assigned room and stay there?"

"Yes, sir," mumbled Leapfrog.

As Leapfrog, Lilith, and Halima slinked off toward Room 108, Conrad slipped away too, hurrying to get there before they did.

Conrad climbed back into his sleeping bag just before Leapfrog came through the door, followed by Lilith and Halima.

He didn't hear another sound from them, but he still couldn't sleep. It seemed to Conrad that hours went by, but still no sleep.

Then he heard a noise, and it wasn't a toy dinosaur or Leapfrog this time. It sounded like the engine of a big truck. Could it be Officer Diaz, coming back to check on them? No, Officer Diaz wouldn't be driving a truck. He drove a patrol car.

Conrad heard clanks and rattles as the sound moved slowly toward the back of the school.

Definitely a truck, thought Conrad. But why would somebody be driving a truck into the school yard in the middle of the night?

Conrad decided to investigate.

He tiptoed out into the hall and moved quickly toward the computer lab at the back of the school building. He peeked through the door of the lab. There were large windows all along the back wall of the computer lab. A streetlight cast soft shadows into the room.

Conrad was right. It was a truck, a big boxy truck. Two men in dark clothes were climbing out of it. One man carried a flashlight. The men came up to one of the large windows and looked in. The flashlight beam darted around the computer lab. Then it flashed right into Conrad's eyes. He blinked and ducked down.

His heart pounded. Did they see him? What would they do if they *did* see him? What were they doing now? Slowly, Conrad rose up and peered through the window again.

The man with the flashlight was pointing to a computer. The other man nodded and pointed to another computer.

They're planning to steal our computers, Conrad thought angrily.

The men were now tapping the windows. Conrad could tell they were trying to figure out how to get in.

One of them went back to the truck and came back with a small saw. He held the saw up to the window. The other man shook his head and said something. They both nodded and then hurried back to the truck.

Conrad saw the lights on the truck come on. Now what kind of dumb

thieves would turn on the lights? he wondered. But did the thieves know that more than one hundred people were asleep in the school? Not likely.

The rear lights on the truck lit up the license plate: STE 499.

The truck drove away. But he was sure the thieves would be back. They

probably were going to get a glass cutter so they could get in through a window.

Conrad ran to the school office. He found Mr. Porter asleep on a cot.

"Mr. Porter, wake up!" Conrad whispered.

The principal just grunted and rolled over.

"Please wake up, Mr. Porter!" Conrad said, and he shook Mr. Porter's shoulder.

"Huh? What? Who is it?" Mr. Porter yawned and squinted at Conrad. "Oh, it's you, Conrad. You kids sure are busy tonight."

"I heard a truck," Conrad blurted out. "And I saw robbers, and they had a flashlight, and—"

"Hold on now, Conrad," said Mr. Porter, sitting up. "I hope this isn't another 'emergency' like the ones we had earlier."

"Oh, no, sir. It's a *real* emergency this time!" Conrad said urgently. "Two thieves were here. They were going to steal our computers. They left, but I know they're coming back!"

"Now calm down, Conrad," said Mr. Porter. "Maybe it was just a bad dream."

"But they tried to get into the computer lab!" Conrad said. "I saw them!"

"Do you spend many nights away from home, Conrad?" asked Mr. Porter kindly.

"Um...well, no," Conrad replied.

"Well, you know, it's normal to have bad dreams when you're away from home," said Mr. Porter.

"But it *wasn't* a dream!" Conrad was getting desperate. "I saw a truck! We should call the police, Mr. Porter!"

"Okay, okay," said Mr. Porter, rubbing his eyes. "Let's say you did see a truck.

Can you tell me what kind of a truck it was?"

"Um...a *big* truck," Conrad said.

"Anything else?"

"Well, not really," said Conrad. "It was just a...a big truck."

"Uh-huh. Listen, Conrad," said Mr. Porter as he lay back down on his cot, "I'm sorry, but I'd feel awfully silly calling the police to report 'a big truck.' Now, why don't you go on back to sleep."

Then he rolled over and went back to sleep himself.

CHAPTER 6
A Special Award

Back in Room 108, Conrad didn't even try to sleep. He had to listen for the thieves. But what if they did come back? He wouldn't be able to stop them. And they might be dangerous. He was just a kid, after all, and a short kid at that.

Why wouldn't Mr. Porter believe him? Well, maybe it was because that crazy Leapfrog had locked him in the food supply room. Or maybe Mr. Porter was just too sleepy to understand that it was a real emergency this time.

Or *maybe* it was because Conrad had forgotten to tell Mr. Porter something important.

Conrad was out of his sleeping bag in two seconds. He tiptoed out of the room and ran to the office.

"Mr. Porter! It's me again," said Conrad. "Wake up, Mr. Porter!"

"What is it now, Conrad?" Mr. Porter was awake, but he didn't sound happy about it.

"I forgot to tell you something," Conrad said. "Something important."

"And I suppose you're going to tell me what that is," sighed Mr. Porter.

"I got the license plate number for the truck!" Conrad said. "It's STE 499."

Mr. Porter was quiet for a moment. "STE 499, huh?" he said. "Are you sure that was the number?"

"Yes, I'm sure," Conrad said.

Mr. Porter was silent again. Then he said, "Okay, Conrad, I'm going to think about this. Meanwhile, you had better get back to bed."

"Well, don't think too long," Conrad pleaded. "I know they're coming back!"

"Go to sleep, Conrad," said Mr. Porter firmly.

Feeling helpless, Conrad walked slowly back to Room 108. *I'm going to think about this.* Mr. Porter just wanted to get rid of me, thought Conrad. He's not really going to think about it. He's not going to do anything at all.

Conrad couldn't stop thinking about what he had seen. The thieves could be back any minute, and if they didn't come back tonight, they'd be back another night. And they would get the computers because no one would believe they had been there the first time.

Conrad finally fell asleep as morning light began to fill Room 108. Not much later, he awoke to Mrs. Akbar's voice.

"Good morning, everyone!" she called out. "I hope you all had a good night's sleep. When you're ready, you can go down to the cafeteria for juice, milk, and cinnamon buns."

But all Conrad could think about was the truck, the thieves, and the computers— and how Mr. Porter hadn't believed him.

"What's wrong, Conrad?" Jasmine was stuffing her blanket and pink pillow into her shopping bag.

Conrad wondered if even Jasmine would believe him. But as they walked to the cafeteria, he told her all about the computer thieves.

"This is serious!" Jasmine said. "Those guys could take all of our computers!"

"I know," said Conrad glumly. But he felt a little better. At least Jasmine believed him.

Now Mr. Porter's voice boomed out over the loudspeakers: "Good morning, students. Will everyone please come to the cafeteria right away. We have an important announcement." He sounded serious.

Jasmine and Conrad walked to the cafeteria together. Conrad saw Officer Diaz standing next to Mr. Porter. Why was he here? To tell kids not to call the police during a school sleepover? Conrad felt more miserable than ever.

Mr. Porter and Officer Diaz were whispering together. Then Mr. Porter said, "Students, Officer Diaz has something important to say to you."

"Good morning," said Officer Diaz. "I hope some of you slept well.

"I am here this morning to give a special award to a student who has performed a great service.

"There was an attempted theft here at the school last night. But due to one student's quick thinking, the thieves have been caught."

Then he explained that a student had heard a truck during the night and had seen the thieves outside the computer lab. This student had gotten the license plate number of the truck and had told Mr. Porter what he saw. Mr. Porter had

called the police, patrol cars were alerted, and the thieves were picked up. Their truck was packed with things they had already stolen.

"And now, Conrad," Officer Diaz continued, "please come up to the front and accept this award."

Conrad blushed as all eyes turned toward him. He walked to the front of the room, smiling all the way. Officer Diaz gave him an official-looking certificate that said he was a brave and responsible citizen.

Everyone in the cafeteria clapped and cheered: "Yay, Conrad! Great job! Hip-hip-hooray!"

"I'm very proud of you, Conrad," said Mr. Porter. "I'm sorry I didn't believe you at first."

"That's okay, Mr. Porter," said Conrad.

As Conrad walked back toward Jasmine, he went past Leapfrog, Lilith, and Halima.

Lilith said, "You're pretty smart, Conrad!"

Halima said, "Way to go, kid."

Even Leapfrog had something to say.

"Hey, Conrad," Leapfrog said, "how about you teach me how to use computers, and I'll teach you how to shoot baskets. Deal?"

"Deal," Conrad said.

Jasmine didn't need to say anything to Conrad. She just smiled.